D0994986

The Man
Whose Mother
Was a Pirate

There are lots of Early Reader
stories you might enjoy.

Look at the back of the book or,
for a complete list, visit
www.orionbooks.co.uk

The Man
Whose Mother
Was a Pirate

by
Margaret Mahy

Illustrated by
Margaret Chamberlain

Orion
Children's Books

The Man Whose Mother Was A Pirate was originally
published in 1985 by J.M. Dent & Sons
This edition first published in Great Britain in 2013
by Orion Children's Books
a division of the Orion Publishing Group Ltd
Orion House
5 Upper Saint Martin's Lane
London WC2H 9EA
An Hachette UK Company

1 3 5 7 9 10 8 6 4 2

The Orion Publishing Group's policy is to use papers
that are natural, renewable and recyclable products and
made from wood grown in sustainable forests.
The logging and manufacturing processes are expected to conform
to th environmental regulations of the country of origin.

A catalogue record for this book is available from the British Library.

ISBN 978 1 4440 0925 5

Printed and bound in China

www.orionbooks.co.uk

There was once a little man who had never seen the sea, although his mother was an old pirate woman.

The two of them lived in
a great city far, far from the
seashore.

The little man always wore
a respectable brown suit and
respectable brown shoes. He
worked in a neat office, and wrote
down rows of figures in books,
ruling lines under them.

Well, one day his mother said, "Shipmate, I want to see the sea again. I want to fire my old silver pistol, and see the waves jump with surprise."

"Oh, Mother!" said the little
man. "We haven't got a car, or a
bicycle, or a horse. And we've no
money, either. All we have is a
wheelbarrow and a kite."

"We must make do!" his mother answered sharply. "I will go and load my pistol and polish my cutlass."

The little man went to work.

"Please, Mr Fat," he begged
his boss, "please may I have two
weeks' holiday to take my mother
to the seaside?"

"I don't go to the seaside!" said Mr Fat crossly. "Why should you?"

"It is for my mother," the little man explained. "She used to be a pirate."

"Oh, well, that's different," said Mr Fat who rather wished he were a pirate himself.

"But make sure you are back in two weeks, or I will buy a computer."

So off they set, the little
man pushing his mother in the
wheelbarrow, and his mother
holding the kite.

His mother wore a green scarf
and gold earrings. Between her
lips was her old black pipe, behind
one ear a crimson rose.

The little man wore his brown suit
buttoned, and his brown shoes
tied. He trotted along pushing the
wheelbarrow.

As they went, his mother talked about the sea. She told him of its voices.

"It sings with a booming voice and smiles as it slaps the ships. It screams or sadly sighs. There are many voices in the sea and a lot of gossip, too.

Where are the great whales sailing? Is the ice moving in Hudson Bay? What is the weather in *Tierra del Fuego*? The sea knows the answers to a lot of questions, and one wave tells another."

"Oh yes, Mother," said the little man whose shoes hurt him rather.

"Where are you off to?" asked
a farmer.

"I'm taking my mother to the seaside," said the little man.

"I wouldn't go there myself," said the farmer.

"It's up and down with the waves, in and out with the tide. The sea doesn't stay put the way a good hill does."

"My mother likes things that don't stay put," said the little man.

Something began to sing in the back of his mind.

"Could that be the song of the sea?" he wondered, as he pushed the wheelbarrow. His mother rested her chin on her knees.

"Yes, it's blue in the sunshine,"
she said, "and it's grey in the rain.
I've seen it golden with sunlight, silver
with moonlight and black as ink at
night. It's never the same twice."

They came to a river.
There was no boat.

The little man tied the
wheelbarrow to the kite. A wind
blew by, ruffling his collar, teasing
his neat moustache.

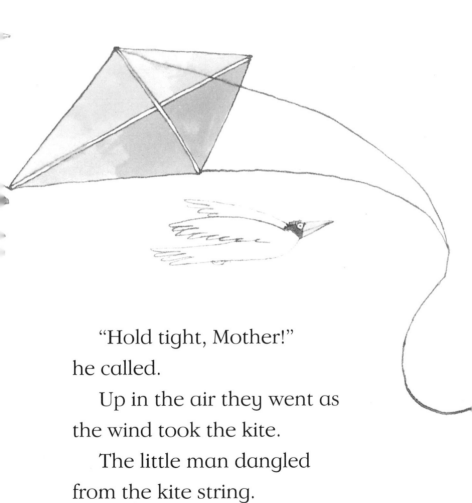

"Hold tight, Mother!"
he called.

Up in the air they went as
the wind took the kite.

The little man dangled
from the kite string.

His mother swung in her wheelbarrow-basket.

"This is all very well, Sam," she shouted to him. "But the sea – ah, the sea! It tosses you up and pulls you down. It speeds you along, it holds you still. It storms you and calms you. There's a bit of everything in the sea."

"Yes, Mother," the little man said. The singing in the back of his mind was growing louder and louder.

As he dangled from the kite string the white wings of the birds in the sky began to look like the white wings of ships at sea.

The kite let them down gently
on the other side of the river.

"Where are you going?" asked
a philosopher fellow who sat
reading under a tree.

"I'm taking my mother to the sea," said the little man.

"What misery!" cried
the philosopher.

"Well, I didn't much like the
idea to start with," said the little
man, "but now there's this song
in the back of my mind. I'm
beginning to think I might like the
sea when I get there."

"Go back, go back, little man," cried the philosopher.

"The wonderful things are never as wonderful as you hope they'll be. The sea is less warm, the joke less funny, the taste is never as good as the smell."

"Hurry up! The sea is calling,"
shouted the pirate mother, waving
her cutlass from the wheelbarrow.

The little man trundled his
mother away, and as he ran he
noticed that his brown suit had
lost all its buttons.

Then something new came into the wind's scent.

"Glory! Glory! There's the salt!" cried his mother triumphantly.

Suddenly they came over
the hill.

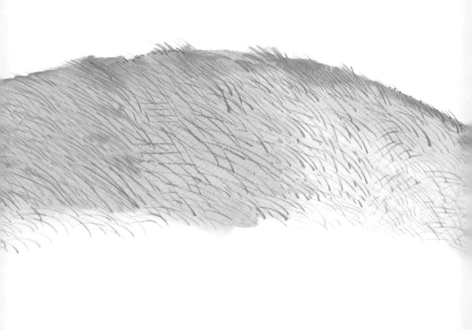

Suddenly there was the sea.

The little man could only stare. He hadn't dreamed of the bigness of the sea. He hadn't dreamed of the blueness of it. He hadn't thought it would roll like kettledrums, and swish itself onto the beach.

He opened his mouth, and
the drift and the dream of it, the
weave and the wave of it, the
fume and the foam of it never left
him again.

At his feet the sea stroked
the sand with soft little paws.

Farther out, the great, graceful
breakers moved like kings into
court, trailing the peacock-
patterned sea behind them.

The little man and his pirate
mother danced hippy-hoppy-
happy hornpipes up and down
the beach.

The little man's clothes blew about in the wind, delighted to be free at last.

A rosy sea captain stopped to watch them.

"Well, here are two likely people," he cried. "Will you be my bo'sun, Madam? And you, little man, you can be my cabin boy."

"Thank you!" said the little man.

"Say, 'Aye, aye, sir!'" roared the captain.

"Aye, aye, sir!" replied the little man just as smartly as if he'd been saying, "Aye, aye, sir!" all his life.

So Sailor Sam went on board with his pirate mother and the sea captain, and a year later someone brought Mr Fat a green glass bottle with a letter in it.

"Having a wonderful time," the letter read. "Why don't you run off to sea, too?"

And if you want any more moral to the story than this, you must go to sea and find it.

What are you going to read next?

More adventures with

or go to sea with

Horrid Henry,

or into space with

Poppy the Pirate Dog,

You could have fun on

Cudweed.

A Rainbow Shopping Day,

or explore

Down in the Jungle,

but watch out for

A Creepy Crawly Story!

Make magic with

The Three Little Witches,

and have
a ball
with

Princesses.

Or follow the star in

The First Christmas.

Enjoy all the Early Readers.